1

Fanny Grace, seated beside her special friend Millie King, looked up from the rough old double desk scarred with hundreds of initials. The new teacher had finished calling all the names, and now she was about to set the morning's work. It was the first day of school in September.

"I want everyone from the second to the sixth grade to write a letter telling how you spent the summer holidays," Miss Thatcher said brightly.

Oh, no, Fanny almost groaned aloud. Teachers were all the same. They made you pay for every holiday you got. Besides, they weren't really interested in what you had done. All they wanted was to find fault with your writing and punctuation, spot all the words you didn't spell to their liking, and make you write them out twenty or thirty or fifty times each. Fanny was wondering if this would be a twenty or a fifty teacher, when she realized that Miss Thatcher was still speaking.

"In the top right-hand corner of the letter you must put your address and the date. Can anyone in grade two tell me what to write here?"

There was no answer. "What about you, Marion? What is your address?" She paused. "Where do you live?"

"Right next to Uncle Sam Marsh, Miss," answered little Marion brightly.

"But I mean in what place?"

"In my house, Miss."

"I want to know the name of this community where we all live," insisted Miss Thatcher. "Can anyone in grade two tell me?"

Fanny scowled. She could see no need for the little ones to know that. None of them ever went anywhere or wrote any real letters, so what was the point in telling them they lived in Famish Gut? She almost wished she didn't know herself, it was such a horrible name. Famish Gut — she hated the sound of it.

Miss Thatcher had gone on to grade three, and one of them had given her the answer. But she wasn't satisfied, oh, no! Now she wanted someone to come up and write it on the board. No one volunteered.

"Then I shall put it here in large letters, with the date underneath." The teacher turned and wrote on the board, "Famish Gut, Newfoundland, September 2, 1929." She faced the children. "Every day you will all write your address and the correct date on the first page that you use in your scribbler," she announced.

Oh, no, thought Fanny, I can't! Not Famish Gut every day, I just can't. Sometimes when her grandfather didn't feel well he said, "A pain in my gut, that's all." Fanny thought he could just as well have said stomach, but she didn't dare tell her grandfather that. Instead she tried not to hear. And now she was condemned to writing Famish Gut every morning. The thought almost made her sick, or gave her a pain in the stomach, to say the least.

But there was no way out that she could see. She rolled her big brown eyes at Millie, sighed, and picked up her pencil. She'd have to write to Aunt Emily, her mother's sister who had gone to Boston to work.

For a moment she was tempted to make up a glorious summer. She'd say that she had gone on a train to St. John's, that she'd been in a huge building with red velvet seats, and she'd watched a moving picture, but there she stopped. Everyone in the school knew she had never been on a train or seen a moving picture. Besides, her mother would check her work and read that letter, and then there'd be trouble. She'd be punished for telling lies. So, with another sigh, she settled down to write the bare truth.

Dear Aunt Emily — then she remembered the hated name, so she started again.

Famish Gut,
Newfoundland
September 2, 1929

Dear Aunt Emily,

Every day this summer I played with my friend Millie King. We each have two dolls, and on fine days we took them out in the back yard and played house or shop. On rainy days I went next door to Millie's to play Flinch with her and her sisters, Helen and Dottie. Sometimes we dug for clams on the beach, but we never got any. Once we took off our shoes and stockings and waded out after crabs, but the water was so cold I thought my feet would drop off. (That's a joke, I didn't really.) I hope you like living in Boston and are not homesick.

Your loving niece,
Fanny Grace

She could have written much more about how she and Millie played that they were married ladies living in a beautiful house with about fifty rooms, and their dolls were their handsome children. But all that was private; the two girls never let anyone hear their pretending.

At last it was time for recess. The pupils marched in a proper line out of the classroom, grabbed their jackets or sweaters from the hooks in the porch, then burst pell-mell out the door, the ten and eleven year olds in the lead.

"Let's play ball," shouted Sarah Thorne. "Jane and I will call sides."

Fanny hesitated. Beside her Millie whispered, "We'll have to play, won't we?" There were only ten girls in the two upper grades, and they were all needed to make the teams.

"I suppose so," answered Fanny. "She'll kill us if we don't." They were both scared of bossy Sarah who had a temper to match her carrot hair.

Fanny walked with dragging steps towards the group. "Hurry up," yelled Sarah, "recess will be over before we get started."

Fanny knew what would happen. Just like last year, every girl would be chosen before her. She was right. Gradually the group was divided until at last Sarah said, "I'll have to take Fatty Grace."

Fanny gritted her teeth. She hated to be reminded that she was short and stubby, but she didn't dare say so. Instead, she looked up under her brown bang and sent waves of hatred towards spindly-armed-and-legged, freckled-faced Sarah.

Sarah's team was first up, and she numbered them, starting with herself and ending, of course, with Fanny. That was because as soon as one girl was caught the side had to retire.

The game started well. Sarah threw the ball up, hit it with her fist, and drove it so far that she made second base. Millie's older sister, Helen, hit safely, and so did Betty Fairway, and that brought Sarah in to score. She was delighted, jumping up and down and yelling, "One run! One run!"

Then Millie hit a long low drive that got her safely to first. Fanny stood at the plate, her throat dry and aching. "We're finished now," she heard Sarah say. "Fatty Grace is sure to get out."

She threw the ball up, and swung her fist. To her delight she sent it sailing out into centre field. She ran as fast as she could, her stubby legs pumping up and down.

"Out!" The shout went up, and she knew that someone had caught her fly ball. She didn't turn to meet Sarah's glare, but walked on out into right field.

Only two girls from the other team had hit when the clanging of the bell brought them back inside. Fanny slid into her place beside Millie. "That skinny Sarah," she muttered, "I won't let her bother me. Perhaps if I call her Scarecrow she'll stop calling me Fatty." But she knew she wouldn't dare. I have to play with Sarah this year and the next, she thought, but then we'll go to the senior school at the head of the harbour where there'll be dozens of girls. I'll be able to keep away from her then.

Behind her she could hear Sarah whispering fiercely, "Slowpoke! Fatty!" In front of her on the blackboard the teacher's big round letters shrieked "Famish Gut!" There was no escape. She blinked and blinked to keep back her tears. School was just terrible.

2

When Fanny burst into her house at lunch time she found her mother stirring something in the iron pot on the shiny black kitchen stove and her grandmother sitting in the rocking chair, knitting as usual. "That's it," she announced. "I'm not going to school any more. Never, never again."

"What on earth has happened?" asked her mother. Grandma dropped the half knitted sock in her lap.

"It's everything about school. I'm finished with it. I'm going to stay home and learn to cook and help you."

"Is it the new teacher? Is she very strict?" asked Mother anxiously.

"I don't know about strict, but I don't want to write Famish Gut every day, and I don't want to be the slowest person in the schoolyard, and I hate being called Fatty." Her voice ended in a sob.

"For goodness sake, what a fuss about nothing! I was called Fatty more than once, and it didn't hurt me. And what's wrong with writing the name of the place where you live?" Fanny shook her head. Mother turned to help Grandma out of her chair and over to the table, then she said, "I have to get these clothes on the line if I'm going to get it dry today. You take up two bowls of soup." And out she went.

Fanny looked up, her tears spilling over. "Do as your mother says, child," Grandma's voice was soft and gentle. They sat in silence for a moment, and then Grandma began to talk.

"When I came to this house as a bride more than forty years ago I could walk as fast and do as much work as anyone." She paused, a half smile on her face. "Then I started to get this rheumatism. At first I couldn't believe that my knees and ankles would swell and get stiff, so that I wouldn't be able to walk without help, but that's what happened. When I couldn't manage the stairs, we made the dining room into a bedroom for Grandpa and me — you remember that. I don't like it. I went upstairs to bed all my life and I'd like to go upstairs to bed now. But I can't, and I have to accept that. I can't change it, and there's no point in complaining."

"You mean I have to accept Famish Gut and Fatty and being slow?"

"You have to decide whether you can change them. Then, if you can't, accept them without a fuss."

Fanny thought for a moment. "You think Mom will let me stay home from school?" Grandmother shook her head. "And we can't move away from Famish Gut?"

"My child, where would be go? Our home is here and our vegetable garden and our hay meadow and pasture. Your grandfather was born in this house, and so was your father."

"Suppose I just don't write Famish Gut every day?"

"I expect the teacher would remind you."

"I know. I'll have to write it." Fanny paused. "But I won't say it, even to myself. I'll think about something else."

"That might work," smiled Grandma.

Just then, Fanny heard her brother coming up the lane past the window, whistling as usual. "Jim's home from school."

"Better put his soup on the table and let it cool a bit."

11

Her brother came into the kitchen, slamming the door behind him. "I'm starved, empty, famished," he announced, as he went to wash his hands in the enamel pan on the little stand in the corner. "What do we have?"

"Soup."

"Any turnips in it?"

"A few."

"Fanny, did you take all the turnip out of mine?" He came to the table. "You didn't, and you know I hate turnip. Here." He seized his spoon and scooped five or six chunks of the hated vegetable out of his plate and dumped them into hers. "That's better. I'm famished."

"Why do you have to keep saying that?"

"Because I am, that's why. Frank King and I ran nearly all the way from school, and that's more than two miles, isn't it, Gran?" Grandmother nodded. Jim was thirteen, two years older than Fanny, so he went from their house, which was near the point that formed the north side of the long narrow harbour, all the way west to the senior school. "So I'm starved, empty, famished . Where's the bread?"

Fanny put the crusty loaf with the breadboard and a knife near her grandmother. A moment later she and her brother, side by side, were spooning up the soup rich with chunks of vegetable and meat, and biting into thick white bread generously spread with golden butter. After a moment, she said, "What did you do at recess?"

"Played baseball."

"Were you any good?"

Jim made a face. "I'm all right out in left field, but I can't hit very well. Frank and I are going to practise after school every day so we don't get struck out so often."

Mother came in and joined them at the table, and the talk turned to what happened in the classroom, not the playground.

Fanny was unusually quiet that afternoon. Twice the teacher had to speak to her sharply to bring her mind back to her work.

As they walked home after school, Millie said, "I'll get my dolls and come over after I have a snack."

"Would you play ball instead?" Fanny asked.

"Play ball?" Millie gasped, her blue eyes wide. Fanny nodded. "But you hate playing ball."

"I know, but I have to try to be good at it or I'll listen to that scarecrow Sarah forever. So I'd better practise, Millie, if you'll help me."

"Oh, I can't play any better than you can, so I need to practise, too. I'll be ready in about ten minutes."

After gulping down three slices of bread thickly spread with butter and jam, Fanny went out into the road to meet her friend. They agreed to take turns hitting.

Millie threw the ball up and sent a low bouncer towards the beach. Fanny was panting when she finally picked it up.

"I think that was a home run, Millie," she laughed. Then she threw the ball up and hit it with all her strength. It sailed off in a beautiful curve through the air, straight into Millie's waiting arms. "I always get out that way." Fanny kicked at the dust of the gravel road, blinking back tears.

"Ready?" called Millie. Again the ball was low and bouncing, but this time Fanny managed to catch it on the first hop.

Fanny's second hit was a nice solid one that made her palm sting, but it sailed right into Millie's arms also. She said nothing. But when the same thing happened five times in a row, Millie said, "That's no good; you get caught out every time."

"I know," sniffed Fanny.

"Try to hit the ball down. While it's bouncing, you have a chance to make first base."

"Millie, I can't."

"Yes, you can. Try to get your hand on top of the ball and think down, down, down."

Fanny tried, again and again. Millie refused to take a turn, she just kept catching the ball and throwing it back. Fanny wanted to quit, but her friend wouldn't let her. Finally she managed to hit the ball into the dirt.

"You did it! You did it!" shrieked Millie, jumping with delight. "Do it again, quick before you forget how."

"I don't even know how I did it." But she tried again and again, until her ball seemed cured of wanting to sail into the nearest fielder's open arms every time.

"Let's go into my house and have hot muffins and tell Gran," invited Fanny.

Next recess, when her turn came to hit the ball, she kept saying to herself "Down, down, down." She made a lovely low bouncing drive past two fielders who had no idea where the ball was, they were so used to looking up. Delightedly she made second base.

"My land, what's happened to Fatty?" yelled Sarah. "She made a safe hit. Someone run up the flag." For once Sarah's rude teasing made no impression.

But her joy didn't last long. Her next low ball was no surprise to anyone, and her short legs didn't get her to the base in time. Sarah was furious. "Why can't you get those stumps of yours to move, Fatty? You belong in the babies' yard."

14

Fanny tossed her head and walked out into right field, pretending she didn't mind making her team out, as usual.

But after school she said to Millie, "I'll have to learn to run faster."

"Then we'll practise running instead of hitting today," answered her friend without hesitation.

"Oh, Millie, will you? I was going to run by myself, but it will be lots more fun with you. No, not fun, but it won't be so horrible."

"See you in ten minutes, then."

As usual, Fanny greeted her mother and grandmother, gulped down three slices of bread and jam, and ran out to join her friend. They marked off a space which they judged to be about the distance to first base, and with a one-two-three they raced off side by side. Millie quickly drew ahead. They paused a moment, and were off again.

By the sixth run Fanny could hardly breathe for the stitch in her side. Millie was hardly out of breath at all.

"I think it's because I'm thinner than you," Millie said.

"I wonder why."

Millie laughed. "Just skinny by nature, I suppose."

Fanny found her grandmother alone in the kitchen when she went in, so she talked about her short legs and her lack of breath. "And look at Millie. She's not much taller than me, but she's thin and can run faster."

"Millie is like her father's people. They're all tall and thin. Her grandfather's nickname was Long John. But your grandfather and father are both big men, and your mother is a big woman."

"I'm not big; I'm only wide." She paused. "How come you're so thin, Grandma?"

"Because my parents were thin, I suppose. And since I haven't been able to move around much, I don't eat all I could. If I put on much weight, I might have to stay in bed, because your mother couldn't pull me out of the chair."

Fanny threw her arms around her grandmother. "Don't do that," she whispered.

Grandma laughed. "As for you, if you want to race up and down the road, you'd better not eat beforehand."

"No snack after school?" Fanny asked, horrified. "I'll try it tomorrow and see. Run first and eat after."

That day Fanny thought she didn't get quite so out of breath, and she was able to do ten runs before a sharp pain stabbed her side. After a short rest, she and Millie ran again.

She was hot and breathless and hungry when she went home. Mother was just taking a pan of rolls out of the oven. Fanny's mouth watered as she washed her hands.

"Supper will be ready in half an hour, but you can have a couple of hot buns to tide you over," said her mother.

"Will you help me get the tangle out of my wool first?" asked her grandmother. Of course, she couldn't say no. But it wasn't a little tangle; it was one that kept her holding here and holding there while her grandmother passed the ball through, and looked, and passed the ball through again. Before they got that tangle all straightened out, dinner was on the table. And for days, every time she was nearly ready to sit down to her hot rolls or bread and jam, Grandma needed a little bit of help, and she never got an afternoon snack at all.

3

The next week Fanny had to help in the potato garden. She began to grumble about having to miss her ball practice, but her mother said sharply. "I don't ask you to do anything except your homework. But this one week, when I'm getting the potatoes out of the ground, I must have help from you and Jim. You might just as well smile as frown about it."

Each day after school, once she had built up the fire under her grandmother's watchful eye, she went out to the back garden. Her mother had dug row after row of brown-skinned potatoes which were lying on the earth, drying in the sun. Fanny took her pail and started to pick up the first ones that had been dug that morning. When the pail was as heavy as she could carry, she took it to the open hatch and tipped it, letting the potatoes rumble into the underground cellar. Mom stopped digging and began to pick up, and soon Jim joined them to help. When the potatoes were safely stowed away, they pulled the withered stalks from more rows, all ready for Mother to start with the shovel the next morning. Before going into the house, Fanny helped her brother bring in junks to fill up the woodbox. By the time she washed her hands and sat at the table, she was almost too tired to eat.

She was glad when the vegetables were all stored away and she could go back to practising with Millie. She knew she could run faster and hit better, but at school she was still the worst player.

In October her father and grandfather finished with fishing and came home for the winter. It was good to sit at the table with all her family; her mother bustled about getting everyone fed, and her grandmother smiled even more than usual.

But the best time was after supper, when the men sat back and lit their pipes, and she and Jim hurried through their lessons. For soon neighbours dropped in and the storytelling started. Nearly every night Uncle Dan and Aunt Lizzie Rourke were there, and Uncle Joe Marsh from further up the road. Millie's father came too, to get out of the way of his eight children all doing different homework, or so he said. The men went fishing on the Labrador in summer, and mended nets and cut wood in winter, just like her father and grandfather.

Fanny sat near her grandmother, with two steel knitting needles and a ball of homespun, practising making nice even stitches. As long as the men talked about elections or government or fish prices, she didn't bother to listen. But when the stories started she let her knitting drop and hung on every word.

One night the talk turned to how soon they'd be going into the woods to start cutting the year's supply of fuel; they had to wait for the ponds to freeze.

"This is going to be a hard winter," said Uncle Joe Marsh, shaking his thin grey hair. "I'm thinking it will be the hardest one for a long time."

"We had a real bitter one back in '98," answered Uncle Dan Rourke. "That was when I was laid up all winter with my broken ankle. "'98, was't it, Lizzie?" Aunt Lizzie nodded without looking up from her knitting.

"There have been bad ones since then, Daniel." That was her grandfather's quiet voice.

"I know that, James. All I'm saying is that '98 was bitter. I'd have frozen to death if you and Joe here and Long John King hadn't found me before nightfall and got me home. I've never been that big a fool since, I can tell you."

"What, not fool enough to break your ankle?" asked Millie's father.

"No, young Willie, but fool enough to forget to feed the fairies."

"Now, Uncle Daniel, you don't believe in fairies," laughed Dad.

"Don't laugh at them, boy. They'll hear you. Yes, I believe in fairies, or the little people, or leprechauns, or whatever you mind to call them. Always carry a bit of bread for them in my pocket when I go into the woods. Then no harm comes to me."

"But you broke your ankle," said Millie's dad.

"So I did, Willie, and you want to know why? I ate all my food that day. I forgot to leave a little bit for them on the ground. I don't know what I could have been thinking of, for I wouldn't choose to anger them. But once my bread was all gone, what could I do? And they punished me alright. They flung me over a big rock, and snap went my ankle."

"Now, Uncle Daniel, you fell."

"No, Willie. I saw this big bare outcrop of rock, and I was going to walk around it, but I could feel myself being lifted up and over and down. I don't know how long I was there on the ground, but when I came to myself I yelled at my old mare to go home. She had sense enough to make

20

her own way back, and that brought the neighbours to find me." The old man shook his head slowly. "It was the fairies that did it; they picked me up and threw me over that rock."

Dad and Willie King looked at each other and smiled, but said nothing. Fanny couldn't tell from the expression on her grandfather's face what he thought, but Uncle Joe was nodding, his eyes half closed.

"Fairies have lots of ways to play tricks on people,' went on Uncle Dan. "I've heard of men being led astray, led miles from where they meant to be, just because they angered the fairies."

"I know men who've been lost in the woods," said Dad. "But that was their own fault." Uncle Dan grunted. "When a man thinks he's lost, he tends to panic. Then he goes around in circles."

"The fairies lead him that way."

"Anyone can tell east from west as long as he can see the sun," Dad went on, not noticing the interruption. "And at night, if he has any sense, he builds himself a shelter and waits for daybreak. Instead of doing that, a man who's a bit scared will rush around without taking his bearings."

"Bedtime," said Mother softly. Fanny rose slowly and reluctantly, still listening to the talk about getting lost and finding your way back, kissed her grandmother, and went out. Soon after she was settled, her mother came up and sat on the edge of the bed to hear her prayers. She was allowed to say them in bed because of the cold.

After she had finished, she asked quickly. "Mom, are there really fairies in the woods?"

"Uncle Dan and his stories!" snorted Mother. "Don't listen to his nonsense."

"Well, he wasn't joking, was he? He really believes in the little people?"

"Well, Uncle Dan is an old man, nearly seventy. His parents came here from Ireland, and they used to talk about leprechauns. He remembers the stories from when he was a little boy. But there's no such thing as fairies, so you don't have to stay awake thinking about them." And her mother kissed her and went downstairs.

Fanny could hardly wait until the next day to tell Millie about how the little people had made Uncle Dan break his ankle because he didn't feed them.

22

"Did he say what they looked like?" asked Millie eagerly.

"No, because my dad and your dad were arguing that there are no fairies. They said he fell."

"Did you ask him?"

"Ask Uncle Daniel?" Fanny shook her head. She wouldn't dare ask questions when the men were talking in her house. After a moment she said, "I wouldn't mind asking Aunt Lizzie. I expect she'd know."

So after school that day, two little girls opened the Rourke's back door, went in, and sat side by side in the kitchen.

"How are you today, Aunt Lizzie?" inquired Fanny.

"Oh, I'm keeping pretty well; can still manage a bit of baking." And a wonderful aroma of spice filled the room as she opened the oven door and took out a pan of brown cookies. "We'll put two or three of these on a plate to cool; then you'll have to give me an opinion."

The girls grinned delightedly at each other. "How is your family, Millie?" went on Aunt Lizzie.

"Fine, thank you."

"None of the children sick?"

"No, Ma'am."

"Here we are. They're cool enough. Try one."

The old woman and the girls sat and solemnly munched the cookies. "Not too much ginger?" inquired Aunt Lizzie.

Fanny shook her head. "They're good." Then she went on, "Is that the kind Uncle Daniel feeds to the fairies?"

"I expect he shares whatever he happens to have. But he's coming in now, you can ask him."

The sound of wood being dumped in the woodbox was heard, and Uncle Dan came in. He didn't look towards the girls, who would gladly have gotten up and crept out, but

23

Aunt Lizzie was saying, "Here's Fanny Grace and Millie King, wanting to find out about the leprechauns."

Uncle Dan frowned at them, then grunted, "The less you bother with the little people, the better."

"We didn't know there were any, Uncle Daniel. What do they look like?"

"How do I know what they look like? A fairy never lets a mortal see him. Some say they're tiny men dressed all in green, with the toes of their boots all curled up, but I don't know. And some say they have pots of gold hidden in the woods, but I never saw any. If I did, mind you, I'd leave them there."

He stopped, thinking, or perhaps seeing the fairy treasure in his mind. "Do you know where they live, Uncle Daniel?" whispered Fanny.

"All through the woods, child, but especially they like a small narrow valley, a kind of glen." He paused. "Why are you asking me this?" He didn't wait for an answer. "You don't want to tangle with the little people. Just share a bit of whatever food you happen to have, and they'll leave you alone. Supper time, isn't it?"

"Goodbye," said Millie, as she darted out the door.

"Thank you," added Fanny, as she ran after her.

Fanny thought a lot about Uncle Dan and the fairies. And when she was writing the hated words Famish Gut, making the capitals F and G as fancy as she could, the words Fairy Glen came into her mind. What a pretty name that would be. And she would't mind at all writing Fairy Glen and the date every day.

4

One day in December Jim came home from school and announced, "I'll need my skates tomorrow; the ice on the pond is ready."

"May as well get Fanny's skates out at the same time," said Mother. So after supper she cleaned and polished the foots and Dad got busy with a flat file sharpening the blades.

How lucky Jim was to be going to the big school, thought Fanny. There was a shallow pond right behind it where they marked off a rink for hockey and one for skating. It would be ages yet before the harbour in front of her home and school froze.

Everyone in Famish Gut went hockey mad in winter. The best men made up a team that played all the nearby outports; they'd been champion for the past three years. The big school had senior and junior boys' and girls' teams, and there was talk of a student competition for the area, too.

Fanny couldn't skate very well. If she tried to go fast or cut a corner, she fell — hard. She could still hear Sarah sneering, "If your bottom had been made of glass, you'd have broken it that time for sure," or "You planning to score goals sitting on the ice, Fatty?" Fanny might pretend to ignore her, but she was hurt and embarrassed just the same.

25

Jim had his troubles, too. He wanted to make the school junior team, but he didn't think he would. He could skate just fine, but he couldn't handle the puck well enough. He'd been working out with the boys for a few days, and he came home discouraged.

"You used to be top scorer on the Famish Gut team, Walter," said Grandmother. "Couldn't you help the boy?"

Fanny looked at her father in amazement. She didn't know he'd been a hockey player.

"Now, Mother, you know I haven't had my skates on since before Jim was born."

"I don't suppose you've forgotten."

Jim looked at his father hopefully. "We'll take the puck out in the back yard tomorrow morning and I'll see if I can spot what you're doing wrong," said Dad.

Next morning Fanny and her grandmother were just finishing their porridge when Jim and Dad came in from outside. They both sat at the table, saying nothing.

"Well?" questioned Mom.

"It's no good without skates and ice," answered Dad. "I'll think about it while Jim's at school."

That morning their father, starting off along the footpath in the direction of Famish Gut Point, came to a small shallow pond. It was not very wide, but there was a straight stretch about forty feet long, frozen solid and smooth. Then he got out his old skates, cleaned the rust off as best he could, and sharpened the edges. When Jim got home from school Dad told him about it and said, "It's no place for playing hockey, but it's big enough for you to stickhandle and shoot, and I'll see what you're doing."

"Can Millie and I come and watch?" asked Fanny.

"No. And you're to say nothing about this outside the family. Jim will have to concentrate and work hard, so there'll just be him and me." Fanny nodded. She understood, really, but she was very disappointed.

Dad and Jim were gone for what seemed like hours on Saturday. "That boy will catch his death of cold," murmured Mother.

"I don't think he'll be still long enough to get cold," answered Grandma calmly.

They came in to their dinner just after noon. Jim wasn't cold, but he was tired. He'd never been on his skates for so long at one time. "That's it for today, son; you're doing better."

"Thanks, Dad. I'm glad you knew that brook was there."

After Jim had gone off to play with Frank King, Dad said, "I think we'll have to get up forty-five minutes or so earlier on school mornings. He needs to get in some practice every day. Could we have breakfast just after seven, Edna?"

"Gracious, it's practically pitch dark."

"We'll get to the brook at quarter to eight; it's light enough then. That will be better than waiting till after school. If he doesn't make that junior team this year, he'll be too old and will have to try for the senior next year; he'd have no chance."

"Oh, I'll have breakfast ready whenever you want it, Walter."

So a new routine started in the Grace house. By the time Fanny came down to breakfast, Dad and Jim had gone. They came back at 8:30: Jim grabbed his books and left for school, and Dad sat and had a second cup of tea.

Only a week later, Jim gleefully announced, "The coach remarked today that my puck control is improving."

"Of course it is," answered Dad.

"That's wonderful," said Mother.

27

Even Grandfather had something to say, though he was usually quiet at the table, concentrating on his food. "You might make as good a hockey player as your Dad some day."

Only Grandma noticed Fanny brush the back of her hand across her eyes, but she said nothing.

Fanny helped with the dishes, for it was Friday evening, and her mother wanted to make a batch of bread before anyone came. She noticed that Dad had the job of helping Grandma get the tangles out of her wool this time.

When she got her schoolbooks and sat down, Dad came close and took her hands. "Going skating on the pond tomorrow?"

"I guess so." Her tears spilled over.

"But why should you cry about that, Fanny?"

"I fall down so much and people laugh at me."

"How would you like to come skating on the brook with me tomorrow?"

"Daddy, you mean it?"

"How early can you be ready?"

"Any time you say."

"Well, since it's not a school day, nine o'clock should be early enough."

Skating with Dad was such fun! She couldn't fall down as long as she was holding on to her father's strong arm. Up and down the narrow strip of ice they raced about twenty times, and then Dad said, "You can skate by yourself. You don't need to hold on to me, but I'll stay near you."

She skated more slowly on her own, but she didn't lose her balance till she tried to turn around. Dad's arm was there, so she didn't sit very hard. Once more, she held on to her father to practise turning and stopping quickly.

When they got back to the house about ten, Mother said, "Millie was here looking for you. I told her you were out with your dad, but you'd be over soon."

Before long the two girls were on their way to the school pond, skates over their shoulders. Almost the first person they saw was Sarah Thorne, who swept by jeering, "Look out for the speed demons." They stayed near the edge of the ice, trying to keep out of the way of the faster skaters. Millie was no better than Fanny, and after about an hour they were glad to take off their skates and go home, get out the dolls, and take refuge in pretending.

Holidays started, with two glorious free weeks. Even the grown-ups in Famish Gut looked upon the twelve days of Christmas as vacation time and did only the work that was absolutely necessary. One day Fanny and Jim and their parents piled into the side sleigh, upholstered in red plush, and drove to the southside to spend the day with Uncle Art and Aunt Rose. Nearly every afternoon neighbours dropped in to visit Grandma, and were served tea and Christmas cake.

But the evenings, when the whole family waited for the janneys to knock on the back door, were the best. After they had tried to guess who the masked visitors were, they settled back to listen to the music of the mouth organ or the accordion, or to cheerful talk. When, as sometimes happened, men her grandfather's age came, the stories were about the old days at sea or at the ice. Fanny especially enjoyed these nights. She knew a good many of Uncle Dan's and Uncle Joe's stories, but the tales of the janneys were usually new to her.

Often they told ghost stories. Even if no one except Uncle Dan seemed to believe in fairies, they all talked as if ghosts were real. Fanny's eyes grew round and she shivered as she

29

listened, but she kept very quiet; she didn't want to be packed off to bed.

One evening Uncle Tom White, an old friend of Grandpa who lived away up near the church, was telling a story. "It was late in the fall and we were on our way back from the Labrador in Skipper Sam Harding's old schooner. We generally made port at night, for you couldn't trust the weather that time of year. But one evening we were caught out on the long stretch of straight shore between Pike's Point and Cape Hard, and the skipper didn't have much choice about staying out. It was a thick night, and the watch was doubled. I knew we must be getting near Shoal Bank, and I was keeping my eyes skinned.

"All of a sudden, I heard a cry, the queerest sound I ever heard in my life. It made my blood run cold. 'What was that?' I said to Jim Barker who was standing near me.

"'I don't know,' he said; 'might be a loon, I suppose.' But I've heard a good many loon cries in my time and I'd never heard one like that before.

"'That's no loon,' I said. And then we saw lights, like the running lights of a ship, off in the distance. At first they seemed to be coming towards us, then they turned suddenly and went out. 'That's Shoal Bank,' I said, 'I'd better tell the skipper.'

"So I made my way to the wheelhouse and reported to the captain what we'd seen. 'My son, what you saw were the lights of a troop ship that was lost there fifty or more years ago. The men's bodies were never found and given a proper burial. It's a warning. We'd better make port if we can at daylight; we're in for a storm.'

"The old man was right, for at the first light we put in to St. Mary's Cove and we'd barely made fast to the wharf

30

before the wind came up. By ten o'clock that morning you couldn't stand upright on the deck."

There were the murmurs from the men when Uncle Tom finished his story, then Dad said, "I can't figure how you got to St. Mary's Cove if that was really Shoal Bank. It's a half day's run in a good time."

"I don't mean St. Mary's Cove in the bottom of the bay," answered Uncle Tom. "It was the one near Cape Hard. I forget what they call it now; they changed the name."

Fanny could feel her heart beginning to pound, not because of the ghost ship, but because they'd changed the name of St. Mary's Cove!

"It's called Harrison's Harbour now. You know it, Walter," he grandfather said. "I suppose the post office or somebody found it confusing to have two St. Mary's Coves in Black Bay so they changed one."

Fanny went to bed that night saying over and over to herself, "They changed the name! They changed the name!" And she fell asleep wondering who changed the name of St. Mary's Cove, and thinking how nice it would be if someone changed the name of Famish Gut to Fairy Glen.

5

The next day at the table, Fanny asked, "Grandpa, who changed the name of St. Mary's Cove to Harrison's Harbour?"

"The government, of course, child; the government in St. John's."

"But why? Who asked them to?"

"Now how do I know? I suppose anyone who thought he wasn't getting his mail because it was being dropped off in the wrong place. Why do you want to know?"

"I just wondered. I thought names of places always stayed the same."

Grandpa grunted and went back to his fish and brewis. As soon as she saw Millie that day, she poured out the story. "So I'm going to write to the Prime Minister and tell him to change the name of Famish Gut."

"You're not!" Millie breathed.

"Yes, I am. I'm going to tell him Famish Gut is an ugly name and we would like it changed to Fairy Glen. But don't you tell anyone; I want it to be a surprise."

Millie promised and Fanny wrote her letter. She just helped herself to some paper and an envelope from a drawer in the kitchen. Mom used them to write to her sister sometimes. But it was four days before she and Millie saved enough to buy a stamp. They mailed the letter addressed to "The Prime Minister, St. John's," without letting even the post mistress see the address.

Every day of the Christmas vacation started out like Saturday. Dad wasn't busy, so first he and Jim went off to the brook to clear off any snow that had fallen, and to practise stick handling and shooting. After about an hour Fanny arrived, put on her skates, and whizzed back and forth over the ice, holding on to her father.

She did this for three days, and then she said, "Dad, I have a very big problem."

"To do with skating?" She nodded. "Tell me."

"It's just that I've never had a secret from Millie. And every morning when she calls for me, I'm up here with you, and I can't tell her that. Besides, Millie falls down as much as I do. Soon I'll be a good skater and Millie won't, and I don't like that."

"I see. What would you like to do about it?"

"I'd like Millie to come up here with us," she whispered.

"But Fanny, there are eight children in the King house. Suppose they all want to come?"

"They won't. Helen and Dottie can skate well already, and Floss is too young to have skates. So there'll be just Millie and me."

"Oh, all right," he smiled. "Invite Millie."

That evening at supper Dad said, "Fanny is bringing a friend to skate with us from now on." Jim looked up and scowled. "I know I said I didn't want anyone else on that scrap of ice with us, but there's room for Millie. Fanny wants her to be a good skater, too."

"I've been worried about Frank," said Jim. "He needs help,

too. Can his dad play hockey?"

Grandpa snorted. "There's your answer, son," said Dad.

"If I get on the team, I'd like Frank to be on it too."

"You want to ask Frank to practise with us?"

"Could I?"

"I don't really mind. It might be better to have two. But I'm warning you, that's it. I'm not coaching any hockey team, I haven't time."

So the Christmas holidays sped by. The girls skated every morning with Dad, and every afternoon by themselves on the little brook. They never went near the big pond to have Sarah and Jane jeer at them.

The vacation was over and they were back at school before the answer to Fanny's letter came. On mail days, twice a week, Jim stopped at the post office on the way home from school to ask if there were any letters for the Grace family. Fanny had already told him, "If you get one for me, it's a secret. I'll tell you about it later, but don't let anyone see my letter."

She was outside with Millie and Floss making a snowman when Jim slyly handed her a letter. She slipped it quickly into her pocket.

"You look frozen, Flossie," said Millie. "We'll finish this if you want to go home."

"My toes are pretty cold," admitted Floss, and away she trudged.

The two friends hurried off behind the barn, and Fanny opened her letter and read it aloud.

Dear Miss Grace,

The Prime Minister has asked me to answer your letter of January 3, 1930 about changing the name of your community. I am to inform you that a petition bearing the

names of two-thirds of the registered voters of Famish Gut
is needed before the government can consider any action.

Yours truly,

P.J. Maner,

Dept. of Marine and Fisheries

Together they puzzled over the letter. They knew what
a petition was, but who were the registered voters? Fanny
decided to ask her grandmother.

"That means all the grownup people living here, the men
over twenty-one and the women over twenty-five who vote
to elect a new government." Fanny nodded. "Why do you
want to know?"

"Oh, we came across it in our reading, and Millie and
I weren't sure what it meant."

"Why didn't you ask the teacher?"

"Oh, Gran, the teacher asks the questions in school, and
then, if you don't know, she tells you." Grandma looked
unconvinced, so Fanny hurried away.

Carefully she lifted the middle leaf from her scribbler so
that it couldn't be missed, and on the page she wrote:

To the government,

We would like the name of this community changed from
Famish Gut to Fairy Glen.

Signed:

She thought about how she could get enough names.
She didn't know how many registered voters there were in
Famish Gut, but she figured that if she went to every house
she could keep track of how many refused, and she could
judge whether or not she had two-thirds.

"We'll do it on Saturday afternoon," she said to Millie.
"We'll take our skates and walk up to the pond. Then we'll

start at the nearest house there and walk back towards home, asking at every door if they'll sign our petition."

Millie looked puzzled. "Why don't we start at our own houses and walk west?"

"Because I don't want our families to know what we're doing till we get enough signatures. I want to surprise them."

So on Saturday afternoon the two girls walked up a lane near the pond to a big white house and knocked at the back door. A pleasant looking older woman answered, and Fanny held out her petition and began to explain what they wanted.

The woman interrupted, "You're wasting your time here, child. Neither my old man nor I can read." And she closed the door.

"Maybe she had grownup sons and daughters," said Millie, as they walked back down the lane to the road.

"She would have called them if she did," answered Fanny. "So that's two I'll have to check under 'No.'" She made two marks on a scrap of paper, and they turned into the next house.

"Sign a petition," said the thin woman, her brown hair falling down her back. "My husband would kill me. He says the less we have to do with government, the better."

"Are you the only grownups here?" asked Millie timidly, for it was her turn.

"There's my husband's old mother, but you won't get her to sign anything. She hardly knows daylight from dark."

So Fanny made three more marks in the No column, and they walked on.

The girls soon began to get discouraged. No one wanted to sign their petition. People gave the most foolish excuses, Fanny thought. One woman said that if she signed, the government might come after her for money. Another said she couldn't sign because she didn't really belong to Famish Gut; she only came there after she was married. One young woman said that if there was a petition to make people keep their goats home, so she wouldn't have to be chasing strays out of her garden every time her children left the gate open, she'd sign that. Then she laughed, showing her crooked yellow teeth. More than one person said that Famish Gut had always been the name of the place, and it was good enough for them.

After they'd knocked at twenty doors and Fanny had more than fifty marks under No, they decided to stop for the day. "Next Saturday we'll start at the school and work our way over to the south side. I expect people will be more sensible over there," said Fanny.

But the next morning her grandfather was in a rage when he got home from church. "What's this I hear about you carrying around a petition?" he asked sternly.

Fanny was taken aback. She had never thought when she had been answering questions about who she was that all of the people knew her grandfather. "It was to ask to have the name of the place changed," answered Fanny, scared almost to death.

"That's what I heard, but I didn't believe it," he bellowed. "What put that idea into your head?"

"I had a letter about it from the Department of Marine and Fisheries. I had to get two thirds of the registered voters to sign a petition."

"To change the name of the place? Whose idea was that?"

"Mine," answered Fanny as bravely as she could. "Famish Gut is a horrible name. I hate it. Famished means starving, and gut — ugh!" She made a strange face and rubbed her stomach.

"Don't they teach you anything at that school?" he shouted. "A gut is a long narrow strait. Famish Gut is a narrow harbour, and once ships get in between the two points out there they're safe from storms. Perhaps the first sailors who came here thought this was a strait leading into another bay, I don't know. But they were safe here in this harbour. I never heard why they called it Famish; perhaps they were starving when they got here and found wild berries and grains so they could survive. Maybe the first settlers nearly starved the first winter. But for whatever reason, it was Famish Gut when my grandfather and my great-grandfather were born here, and Famish Gut it will stay." He paused, breathing hard, and then went on. "What did you plan to name it?"

"Fairy Glen."

"Fairy Glen!" Grandfather's face was so red, she thought he would explode. "What self-respecting captain in his right mind would take refuge in Fairy Glen?"

"Now, James, that's enough," said Grandmother quietly. "Fanny knows you don't want her to ask anyone else to sign the petition, so you don't need to go on shouting at her." And to Fanny's surprise, though Grandpa still sputtered a bit, he stopped bellowing.

She went to her bedroom and put the petition away among her treasures. When she went back to the kitchen Grandma gave her a special never mind look and glanced down at her own swollen ankles. Fanny knew what she was saying: "We must accept the things we can't change." She sighed, and went off to tell Millie all about it.

6

Soon the ice on the harbour was strong and the young men who had finished school — like Margie Marsh's brother — measured off a full-sized rink for themselves and a smaller one for the children. Twelve girls from the three senior grades in Fanny's school had skates and that was just enough for two hockey teams. So each day when their classes were finished they rushed to their rink for a game.

Sarah bossed everyone, as usual. The first day she was stuck with both Fanny and Millie, and she said, "Fatty Grace, you be in goal; maybe you can stand up there."

"I don't think the same person should be in goal all the time. It's too cold." Fanny was surprised at her own courage, but she knew something Sarah did not. During the past month she and Millie had been skating on their brook for hours each day, and they were no longer awkward. "I don't mind starting in goal, but I'll only stay about twenty minutes."

Sarah looked at her, open-mouthed. At last she replied, "All right. We'll put Millie King in goal after that. But if either of you fall under my feet, don't blame me if my skate cuts you." Fanny waited till Sarah had turned her back before she stuck out her tongue. She really wasn't *that* brave!

And she was terrible in goal. She let the other team score

40

three times, and Sarah was furious. Fanny didn't know whether to be glad or sorry when she finished her turn as goalkeeper. She knew she could skate fairly fast and not fall down, but she hadn't practised with a stick in her hand, and she was afraid that she wouldn't be able to control the puck. She was quite right; it bounced and slid and would not go where she wanted it to at all.

The next morning, as soon as Jim and Frank got off the ice, she and Millie practised under Dad's watchful eye. He showed them how to move the puck along the ice, cradling it with the stick, and he made them pass it to each other dozens of times.

Soon he said, "This is not sensible. You two need to be able to skate much better before you start worrying about a puck."

So they agreed that for a half hour or so each morning they'd skate, learning to carry a hockey stick, to stop and turn quickly, and only after that did they use a puck. In the afternoons they had to try to play hockey, or the teams would be shorthanded, and Sarah would be angry.

Jim and Frank continued to play every morning with Dad and every afternoon at school. Great was their joy when they were both chosen as forwards on the school junior team. Every Saturday the two teams, junior and senior, went to some nearby community — Cheerful Cove, Dent's Bight, or Rocky Harbour — to play the school teams there. And there were plans to take two girls' teams the next year.

The news excited Sarah. "In two years, when I go to the senior school, I'll make the girls' team," she boasted. No one contradicted her: she was a strong fast skater, and she backed away from no one. In fact, thought Fanny, if you got in her way she'd go right over you.

The Famish Gut men's team was very busy, too. They played a series of games with the nearby communities and beat them all to become area champions. That earned them the right to go to St. John's to meet the champions from three other areas. On that play-off day, every child in Famish Gut wanted to stay home from school if there was a radio in their house, or listen at a neighbour's if there wasn't. But of course they were sent off to school in the morning as usual. However, not many men went to cut wood; a man could afford to take one day off.

At lunch time Fanny was greeted with the news that their team had beaten Pike's Inlet. If they could win over Shepherd's Cove that afternoon, they'd be the champions.

"Can I come to your house after school to hear the game?" asked Millie. The Kings didn't own a radio.

"Sure."

"Me, too?" asked Jack Green.

"Anyone can come to my house. We may not all get in, but you can all hear," answered Fanny. So when she ran down the road and into her lane after school half the pupils of the school followed her.

She opened the kitchen door. "Mom, can Millie and...." She stopped, for the kitchen was already full. Her grandparents, her parents, Millie's father and mother, Uncle Dan and Aunt Lizzie, Margie Marsh's parents and grandfather were all there. The only sound in the room came from the radio.

Her mother hurried to the kitchen door and said softly, "Take off your overshoes and creep in and sit on the floor." The children all edged forward. About half of them managed to get into the kitchen, the others crowded into the back porch. "The score is one-one," whispered her mother.

42

The news was passed to the last child near the back door. Then they listened tensely, silently urging their team toward the rival goal, and letting out their breath in little sighs of relief when the enemy was turned back from the Famish Gut goal. The announcer said that there was five minutes left in regulation time.

Fanny gripped her hands so tightly together the knuckles showed white. There was another shot on the Famish Gut goal, and a sigh as the goalie turned it aside. Then the announcer's voice rose in excitement as Jack Miller broke away up the ice and let go a sizzler. "What a save!" the voice exulted. "Wait, there's the rebound. They Score! Number eight, Bill Marsh, has scored and put Famish Gut ahead!"

A great shout went up from the kitchen and the porch. Uncle Joe Marsh stood up and cheered, his face glowing with pride in his grandson. Then he got embarrassed and sat down quickly. There was a buzz of excited talk and laughter as the children hugged each other.

"Quiet! It's starting again," said Grandpa. Silence fell, and the tension was almost unbearable . Each time the opposing team got the puck, Fanny felt a knot twist in her stomach. The five minutes seemed like an hour with the teams racing from one end of the rink to the other. Then came the welcome sound of the buzzer to end the game, and another great shout of triumph went up. Famish Gut was the champion! Even though the children missed greeting the heroes when they arrived home (for that was late at night), they could still yell, "We're the best!" when they met one of their neighbours who was on the team.

Soon after they were warned off the harbour ice for it was developing cracks and breaking into pans that floated out the narrow harbour mouth. For nearly a month they continued skating on the school pond and on their private brook.

Easter holidays came and went, and the school children paid for them by describing them for the teacher. The ice was gone, the road was too muddy for ball, so Millie and Fanny went back to their dolls. But somehow, pretending wasn't as much fun as it used to be.

Then one afternoon when Fanny got home she found her mother bending over a big box of clothes. Aunt Emily had sent the package through the post office. She had a new job and the people for whom she worked had a twelve year old daughter who had outgrown lots of perfectly good clothes.

Aunt Emily thought they would fit Fanny, so she had packed them and sent them, just in case.

"Try this on," said her mother. "I hope it's not too tight."

Fanny pulled on a lovely plaid wool dress. She got it down over her hips, though truth to tell it was pretty tight across her stomach. Then she put on a green coat with a little grey fur collar, and a cap to match.

"It's just lovely," breathed her mother, "and hardly worn at all, except a bit around the buttonholes."

"I may be able to darn that," said Grandma, as Fanny took it off and tried on the other coat, a brown one without fur. It was too long, and rather tight. Then she began trying on the dresses, skirts, and sweaters. About half of them were too tight across the hips.

"I'll be able to wear them, Mom. I'm getting thinner, aren't I, Grandma?" Her mother was already turning them inside out, to see how much material there was that Grandma could let out.

The next day she walked proudly to school wearing her new green coat and cap over her plaid dress which Grandma had let out about an inch around the stomach and hips.

Margie Marsh noticed her new clothes when she was hanging up her coat in the porch and came over to touch the soft fur. "It's not really new, is it?" she asked, as she eyed the darned buttonholes. "I guess your aunt sent that from the States. She's a housemaid for some rich people, isn't she?"

Suddenly all Fanny's pride in her new clothes was gone. Margie was the only girl in her family, so even if her dress was a dyed floursack with Robin Hood still visible across the back, still it was made for her. Besides, she made housemaid sound like a nasty word. Fanny didn't answer.

Margie started again at recess. "The girl where your aunt works must be thinner than you. I noticed where the dress is let out."

Fanny was furious, especially since Sarah heard that remark and cackled, "Everyone is thinner than Fatty Grace."

She stormed home at lunchtime. "I don't want to wear the secondhand clothes," she said.

Her mother looked at her. "Now what's wrong?"

"They made fun because I had to wear secondhand clothes."

"More than half the children in that school wear hand-me-downs," her mother replied.

"It's different when it's handed down in your own family."

"How is it different?"

Fanny shrugged. "I don't know."

Her mother glanced at the pleated skirt Grandma was letting out. "We're lucky my sister works for people who can afford to give clothes away. I only wish they had boys, too. So you'll wear these and ignore any remarks made out of jealousy. I don't want to hear any more about it."

So Fanny went on wearing her new secondhand clothes, and Margie made some remark as each different thing appeared. If Sarah noticed, she said nothing. She wore the same dress every day, and more and more food stains appeared down the front, but she didn't seem to notice. All she cares about is winning, thought Fanny. If ever I could beat her at ball or hockey, perhaps she'd stop calling me by that horrible nickname.

7

Spring came to Famish Gut. The ground was ploughed for the planting of potatoes and other vegetables. The sheep and goats produced their young, and broody hens sat on their eggs. The men went off to the Labrador to spend five months fishing.

This summer was a little different from the others. Fanny and Millie didn't spend all their time playing with dolls. Instead, they got up a ball game in the schoolyard every morning. Millie and her three sisters, Margie, Betty Fairway and her older sister, and Fanny made up the teams. Four wasn't really enough on a side, so they cut out third base and that made things better. Little Floss King was only seven, but no one said anything about her being slow. Sarah and Jane lived much further up the road, and to Fanny's relief they never came to the school yard to play.

Sometimes they had to work in their own back gardens, pulling weeds and bringing water to the tiny plants in a dry spell. When the grass was cut they helped spread it to dry in the morning and rake it into big piles in the afternoon. The gardens were the grandest places to play tag or hide-and-seek then. They ran around the big round piles and buried their faces in the sweet dry hay.

47

In late August the wild raspberries and blueberries were ripe. Fanny always went berry picking three or four times with her mother, and Mrs. King looked in on Grandma every so often to make sure she was all right. Sometimes Mrs. King took Fanny with three or four other of her children, so the Graces had raspberries for jam and blueberries for muffins and pies.

But something special happened about berry picking. Mr. Walters from up near the church arranged to buy berries people had picked. Because it was such a long walk to the barrens, Mr. Walters drove people there and left them for the day. When he returned for them in the afternoon he bought the berries for ten cents a gallon and put them in large wooden boxes in the back of his truck.

Fanny was allowed to go with the King girls and their mother. She was excited for she had never earned money in her life. Even when Sarah Thorne and Jane Miller climbed into the truck, her day was not spoiled.

Mr. Walters left them by the side of the road and drove away. The berries near the road were all picked, so they headed west along little paths between the bushes. When they came to a small clearing, Aunt Maude King said, "Leave your lunches here. It's a good place to boil the kettle at noon. I'll blow the whistle for you. Now scatter and pick."

Fanny left her basket in the clearing and soon filled her mug with blueberries and emptied it into the basket. She did this again and again, never going far from the clearing but picking all the berries from nearby bushes.

At the sound of Aunt Maude's whistle, they hurried back to the clearing. Sarah took one quick look at Fanny's basket and said, "Is that all you picked this morning? Why, there's not five cents worth there. And they're so scrawny and small

I bet Mr. Walters won't even buy them. What were you doing all morning, Fatty? Sitting down?"

"No, I was not sitting down. And it's none of your business, anyway." She grabbed her basket and put it behind her, out of sight.

Fanny ate her lunch — four slices of bread with thick slabs of cheese, and two chewy chocolate cookies, and a mug of scalding tea — and when every crumb was finished she wiped her hands and mouth. She was about to go off picking again when Aunt Maude called her. "Take your basket with you and move away from the clearing," she said quietly. "Just take a few handfuls of the biggest berries from each bush. You'll pick a lot more that way." Fanny nodded and picked up her basket.

This time she didn't bother to glance around and see where Millie and Dottie were, or even if she was within reach of the clearing. She did as Aunt Maude had suggested, pulled a few of the biggest berries from each bush and moved on. She didn't use the little mug, but tied it on her belt. Her basket grew heavier and heavier, but she didn't mind. All she could think of was Sarah's face when she appeared, her basket brimming over with plump blueberries. "I'll show that scarecrow she can't do everything better than me," she muttered.

At last her basket was full. She straightened her back and stretched her arms; she really was stiff and tired. She turned to call out to Millie, but there was no one on her left. She turned all around; not a soul was in sight. Without realizing it, she had made her way down into a shallow valley and the bushes, instead of being knee high, were up to her waist.

Suddenly the thought flashed through her mind: Uncle

Dan's fairies liked to live in valleys. She was in a fairy glen, and she didn't have a morsel as an offering. You couldn't count berries for the little people could pick all they wanted themselves.

What nonsense, she told herself firmly. Mom says there are no fairies; it's just Uncle Dan's funny ideas. I'll climb back up to that ridge and I'll see Aunt Maude and everyone.

Holding the basket carefully, she made her way to a higher place and looked about. But instead of almost level ground dotted with people, she found more little valleys with big rocks sticking up.

The road is this way, said a voice in her mind very clearly, so bravely she started off. But soon she found herself in a tangle of berry bushes and alders, reaching above her head, with hardly any path at all.

This way, this way — it sounded like a chorus of whispers all around her. She put her hands over her ears and looked all about, more frightened than she had ever been in her life. It's the little people! It's Uncle Dan's fairies trying to lead me astray! They might even fling me down and break my leg! she thought.

Fanny almost expected to see a swarm of little people dressed in green. They lead you away from home, Uncle Dan had said. Suddenly she seemed to hear her father's calm voice: "If you're frightened, you go around in circles; you have to get your bearings."

Quickly, almost gaily, she moved to a nearby tree and climbed. I'll be able to see my friends and the clearing, and perhaps the road, she told herself. But the tree wasn't very tall, and when she could climb no higher, she still saw only trees and bushes.

Choking back sobs, she got back to the foot of the tree

and looked about. Suddenly she noticed her shadow stretching away to the left. That's the way, she thought, her heart pounding with relief. This morning, when Millie and I left the road we played stepping on our shadows. So I'll keep my shadow behind me and I'll get back.

She set off, being careful to keep her shadow stretching out behind her. She trudged on bravely, and her shadow grew longer and the light grew dimmer. But nothing looked familiar. In fact, the ground began to get marshy, and she didn't remember her shoes having been damp that day.

The sun rises in the east and sets in the west, Fanny began to sing to herself to keep from feeling scared. Then she sang aloud, "The sun rises in the east and sets in the west." Suddenly she stopped. She hadn't taken into account the fact that the sun had moved. She forced herself to figure this out slowly; she even poked sticks into the ground to represent the road and the sun.

I walked west from the road this morning because I was stepping on my shadow, she thought. But now the sun is in the west, so I should be stepping on my shadow again to get back to the road.

Tears slipped from beneath her lids and down her cheeks. She'd been walking away from the road all this time. She had to turn back. Bravely, she started. This is wrong! This is wrong! The voices in her head started again.

"You hush," she said aloud. "I'm taking my bearings from the sun. I know west from east." And she trudged on, but all the time the voices in her head kept saying, This is wrong!

Fanny left the marshy ground behind her, and the bushes were not quite so high. Gradually her shadow grew fainter and fainter until she could hardly see it. I'd better take my bearings before the sun goes down, she thought. She climbed a nearby tree, looked in the direction of her shadow, and on a slight ridge ahead picked out a tall pine with a spruce growing right beside it. I'll make for that, she decided.

So she did, but before she reached it her shadow had disappeared completely. She kept her eye fixed on the tall tree, not daring to look around. When she reached the tree, Fanny climbed it, as high as she could, ignoring the sticky on her hands and the tears in her dress, but still looking east.

To her amazement, she saw a glow away in the distance, but she couldn't tell what it was. And then she remembered the stories about weird lights that disappeared and were always warnings of trouble. She watched this light for a time, and it didn't vanish. That's east, so I'll walk towards it, light or no light, she decided.

But when she was on the ground again, Fanny couldn't see the glow. She walked on as long as she was sure of the direction, and then climbed another tree. The glow was still there, far ahead, but a little to the right. Again she picked a tree between her and the light and started walking toward it.

The next time she climbed and looked, she was sure the glow came from a fire. And a fire meant people, and it really wasn't very far away.

As she walked on, she fancied she heard someone call her name. She stopped and strained her ears. The sound of "Fanny" seemed to float toward her, and it wasn't at all like the voices inside her head.

"Here I am!" she called, but there was no answer. She went on as fast as she could.

"Fanny?" This time she was sure it was her mother's voice.

"Here I am! she yelled. Then she cupped her hands around her mouth and called as loudly as she could, "Here I am!"

"Keep walking towards my voice!" It really was her mother. "Fanny!"

"Coming!"

"Fanny!"

"Coming!"

They called to each other five or six times, and then she was in her mother's arms. "You gave us an awful fright, child. How did you get separated from the others?"

"I was trying to get a full basket of big berries, Mom. And now I don't know where I left them." Fanny started to cry.

"Never mind berries," said her mother. "Mr. Walters is going to drive us home in his truck." She hurried Fanny toward the fire where Aunt Maude was blowing her whistle to get all the searchers back and where ten or twelve women and big boys called cheery greetings to her.

Before long Fanny was in her grandmother's arms telling the story to her, and to Aunt Lizzie Rourke who had come to keep her company.

"You didn't feed the little people, of course," said Aunt Lizzie. "Maybe you'd better next time, just in case."

Next time, Fanny promised herself, I won't let that Sarah bother me so much that I'll forget to watch where I'm going. I'll never get lost again.

8

School started, and apart from the fact that she was in the highest grade, everything was the same as before. True, she could now hit as well as anyone, except Sarah and Jane, but she was still rather slow. And her nickname didn't change: Jane and Sarah never called her anything except Fatty or Fats, and most of the other girls did the same. She could think of no way to make them stop, so she pretended she didn't mind.

December came, and again the skates were cleaned and sharpened. But when Jim tried his on, he found that his feet had grown so big he could barely squeeze into the boots. He looked from his father to his mother in dismay. "I can't wear them; they're killing me!" His parents didn't answer.

Quickly Fanny put hers on and stood up. "Mine are all right," she announced bravely.

"They seem a bit tight," said Dad.

"They pinch my toes a tiny bit, but I can wear them, honest, I can!"

"Put them away for now. We'll see what we can do," said Mother.

Jim stayed after school next day to help clear a thin layer of snow off the ice on the pond and to mark off a rink. No one mentioned skates when he got home.

On Wednesday Mother went as usual to her Ladies' Aid meeting at the church. The next day she said to Fanny, "After school I want you to try on all the clothes Aunt Emily sent. I'm taking anything that's too small to the church tomorrow. We're planning to have a sale."

So Fanny tried on the dresses, skirts, and coats that had come in three separate parcels from Boston. Some of the clothes were too long and narrow, for though Fanny was thinner she was still a short stocky child. There were more clothes than Mother could comfortably carry. "I'll get Maude King to help me," she said, "and I mustn't forget the two pairs of skates."

"Mom, you can't give away my skates!" exclaimed Fanny.

"I'll get you a pair big enough to wear socks in. Don't worry. You'll have skates."

That afternoon mother showed a handful of tickets cut from cardboard and signed by the secretary of the Ladies' Aid. "We decided on one ticket in exchange for a skirt or sweater, two for a dress, and three for a coat or boots and skates," she said. "I ended up with nearly thirty tickets, so I made Maude King take half. By the time clothes get passed on to the fourth girl or boy in her house, they're not much good to anyone. You and Jim are to come with me tomorrow to try on skates. I might even find a pair of shoes to fit you."

"What did they do about women with big families?" asked Grandma. "Maude has her tickets, but there are plenty others with nothing to turn in."

"Anyone could get a ticket for promising to work three hours scrubbing the church or school. And a load of wood counts two tickets."

Grandma nodded. "That's good. No child should go without, and this way it's not charity."

"I want to be there sharp at nine," Mom said to Fanny. "There weren't as many skates turned in as I expected."

Fanny and Jim both got skates, and Fanny found good black shoes that just fitted. There was even a warm jacket for Jim, and Mom still had four tickets, which she gave to the minister's wife.

When Fanny went into class the next morning, she noticed that two of the younger children had on her dresses. Then she saw that Margie Marsh was wearing one from the box. Even though it had been too long and narrow for her to wear, she recognized it. She didn't know whether to mention it or not.

As they were getting their coats for recess, Margie said, "Did you notice my new dress?"

"It's not new," scoffed Fanny. "That's one my aunt sent from Boston."

"I don't care," answered Margie with a big smile. "It's new to me, and that's real lace on the cuffs and collar. But I'm dying to have a coat with fur like yours. Perhaps my mom will get me one next year."

Fanny was too surprised to speak.

Right away the skating and hockey practice started in earnest. Frank called for Dad and Jim before 7:30 and away they went to check, pass, and shoot. They were so good, Dad said, that he'd soon need help on his side. Fanny and Millie were at the brook wearing their new secondhand skates by 8:15 and they practised carrying the puck, passing, and shooting, all with Dad's help in the mornings and by themselves in the afternoons. Fanny didn't say so, but she intended to be a better hockey player than either Sarah or Jane.

When the rink was ready on the harbour ice, Margie's brother, Warren, offered to coach the girls from their school. They wouldn't play other schools, but they'd get good training and maybe make the junior team at the big school next year. For three or four weeks, he tried everyone in different positions, including goal.

Then one day he said, "Fanny Grace, you're good at getting in front of the goal, and you have a quick wrist shot, so you'll play centre. Millie King, you shoot better from the right side, so you'll play right wing." The two friends smiled at each other; they always practised with Millie on the right.

Warren made up two teams, giving each girl her own position. As well, he had four young girls who were used as forwards to give the regulars a rest. Sarah was told to play defence and she wasn't very happy about that. "I like to shoot and score," she said.

"So you will, sometimes," answered Warren. "But you're the tallest and strongest girl, and you're needed on defence." Of course she's the tallest, thought Fanny; she's older than everyone else.

Millie and Fanny played happily on the forward line with Margie Marsh. Sarah and Jane were on the opposing team.

After a couple of weeks, Warren mixed up the teams, but each girl still played her own position.

Before the ice started to break up, Fanny thought ahead to next year. Six of us will go to the senior school and meet girls from the head of the harbour and the south side. And what will they think my name is? Fatty. If I don't do something to make this crowd stop, I'm going to be called Fatty as long as I live.

She knew Sarah was the leader, but she was afraid to tackle her. She found no answer to her problem as she practised sending the puck along the ice to hit a small stick her father had laid down, or lifted it to sail through a hoop he held waist high. He was really drilling them in puck control. "You have to be able to send the puck exactly where you want it to go," Dad said. "Otherwise you waste your scoring chances."

So for days and days, Fanny and Millie practised shooting, and they became so good Dad praised them, which was unusual. "There won't be a girl on the ice with better control than you two," he said.

Fanny glowed. If I'm as good a player as Sarah, and I know I am, she thought, surely I can find the courage to tell her to stop calling me Fatty. And I'd better do it soon!

That afternoon as the game started, with Fanny, Millie, and Betty Fairway as forwards and Sarah and young Rita Green on defense, Sarah said, "I'm going to play up the ice a bit today, so don't hog the puck, Fatty. Pass it to me as often as you can."

Fanny glared at her. "My name is Fanny, so don't you call me Fatty any more." She was amazed at her own daring.

As for Sarah, she broke into a loud guffaw, her mouth wide open. "How are you going to stop me Fatty?"

She really hadn't any idea, but she answered bravely, "You'll see, and you'll be sorry."

Sarah doubled up with laughter. Then she said, in her bossy way, "Go on and take the face-off, Fatty. He's whistling for you."

Fanny skated over and Warren dropped the puck between her and Hilda. She got the draw, flicked the puck over to Millie, and they raced down the ice. Millie shot, and the goalie turned it aside. Fanny got the rebound and she was trying to get into a good position when she heard, "Here, Fatty, pass it to me! Fatty! Fats!"

She cradled the puck with her stick and looked around. Sarah was on her left, near the goal crease, facing her, open-mouthed. "Pass, Fatty, pass!" For a moment everything was a blur in front of Fanny's eyes.

Almost without realizing what she was doing, she wound up, lifted the puck slightly, and hit Sarah right in the stomach.

Sarah dropped her stick and fell to the ice, her knees drawn up. Warren blew his whistle and hurried over. The girls gathered around, solemn, frightened. "Will she be all right?" asked Jane.

"In a minute, I think." Warren straightened up. "She's just had her wind knocked out, that's all."

Sarah moaned and sat up. Her face looked green. "Take it easy," Warren cautioned. The only answer was another groan.

"You certainly hit her hard," said Jane, giving Fanny a cold stare. There was no answer to that.

Slowly Sarah got to her knees. "I'm fine, don't fuss," she said between clenched teeth. "I'll get off the ice for a minute." Warren helped her to her feet and over to the one old bench where she sat, head hanging. Jane sat beside her, watching, solemn.

"Let's get the game started again." Warren waved in two spares to take the places of Sarah and Jane. They played for less than half an hour, then Warren said it was too dark. "See you tomorrow," he called, as he picked up his puck and started off. "Want me to walk home with you, Sarah?" he paused beside her.

"No, Jane is nearly ready. We'll go together." Sarah still looked pale as death. Soon she got to her feet. Jane took her by the arm and they slowly walked away.

The girls started to take off their skates. "That's the first time any of us have been hurt on the rink," remarked Betty Fairway. "I hope no one tells, or my mother will hear and then she won't let me play any more."

"That's silly," scoffed Margie Marsh. "There'll be a girls' league in the bay next year, a dozen or more teams. Your mother will let you try for the school junior team."

"She won't if she hears anyone got hurt. Warren won't tell your mother, will he?"

"I don't know. Let's try to catch him before he gets home."

"You should have been more careful, Fatty Grace," said Betty crossly. "I expect you've spoiled everything." She and Margie hurried away.

Fanny and Millie walked down the road together. Usually they chattered about the game, but today neither of them said a word except Goodbye as they parted at the King's gate. Fanny's heart felt like a hard cold lump in her chest. Maybe no one else had guessed that she had meant to hit Sarah, but Millie knew. And Fanny Grace knew, too.

9

At supper she had to force herself to answer her family's questions about school and hockey practice. Then, as long as she was busy with homework, she could keep her mind off what she had done. But when her books were put away, and Uncle Dan and Uncle Joe Marsh came in, she found she couldn't listen to their talk. She kept seeing Sarah lying on the ice, or on the bench, without strength enough to sit upright.

Maybe I really hurt her and she won't be able to play any more, Fanny thought. And instead of feeling glad that she might be rid of a hated enemy, she felt very small and very mean. I shouldn't have lost my temper like that. After all, Fatty sounds nearly like Fanny, so what does it matter what she calls me? We both like to play hockey, and that's what counts.

The next morning Millie was still unusually quiet, though she gave her friendly smile when she met Fanny. In the schoolyard there was no sign of Sarah. The bell rang and they hung up their heavy outdoor clothes in the porch. But still Sarah didn't come. And neither did her young sister.

Fanny thought the morning would never pass. Perhaps

she'd find out at recess why Sarah was away. Jane would probably know.

The girls gathered in their own corner of the yard. "I don't know why she's not here," Jane said loudly. "Sometimes she has to stay home to help her mother if one of the young ones is sick. Of course, she may not be able to get up this morning. She got a very hard blow in the stomach yesterday." She glared at Fanny.

"Are you going in to see on the way home?" asked Betty.

"No, I am not. If the kids have some sickness, I don't want to catch it. Besides, what would I say to Mrs. Thorne if Sarah is dead?" Jane spoke in a shocked whisper, and looked again at Fanny.

No one answered. Then Millie spoke up. "We'd better play something or we'll freeze. I'll be it for tag. I'll count to ten; you'd better scatter."

So there was no more talk of Sarah at recess, and of course they didn't talk in school. As soon as they were dressed at lunchtime, Fanny said to Millie, "I forgot something." She hurried back into the classroom, grabbed Sarah's arithmetic book, tucked it under her coat and held it with her left arm. She couldn't wait until the next day to find out, and she had to have some excuse for going to the Thorne's house.

First, she went home and tried to eat, but her throat was so tight she could hardly choke down a mouthful of food. Her mother, busy serving, didn't notice, but Grandma looked at her anxiously.

Fanny rose from the table as soon as she dared. "I have to go back early today," she announced.

Her mother suddenly noticed the barely touched meal. "What's the matter? Don't you feel well ?"

"I'm fine, but I'm in a hurry." She was putting on her coat.

"Are you in trouble at school?" her mother asked, suspiciously.

"No, Mom, but I have to do something special before the bell rings. I have to hurry." And she ran out. Up the road she raced, and knocked at the Thorne's door, her heart pounding.

"Is Sarah sick?" she asked the thin pale woman who answered the door.

"Well, there was something wrong with her last night; she hardly ate a bite. But she seems all right today. The baby and young Ruby are sick, though. Do you want to come in?" Fanny nodded. "Come on, then." She led the way through the back porch and opened the kitchen door. "Here's one of your school friends, Sarah. I'm going to the well and the cellar." She took a coat off the peg, pushed Fanny inside, and closed the door behind her.

Fanny darted a quick look around. The kitchen was dirty and untidy. The curtains at the windows were in tatters, the rag mats on the floor so dirty you couldn't see the pattern. Lines of clothes hung across the kitchen, and the table was loaded with used dishes.

Young Ruby sat on the settle beside the stove, a grey blanket around her. Nearby the baby slept in his crib. Sarah and two little boys sat at the table, eating. Sarah was staring at her in amazement. "I didn't expect to see you."

"I brought over your arithmetic book so you wouldn't be behind tomorrow." She paused. "Don't you feel well?"

Sarah shot a quick glance at the children. Ruby was listening with both ears. "You heard my mother say I'm fine. I'm home to help because the others are sick. You'd better not go close to Ruby. Come over here and show me the arithmetic." She drew Fanny to the far corner of the kitchen,

63

their backs to the children. "Why did you come here?" she hissed.

"I wanted to see if you were all right, and to tell you I'm sorry I hit you yesterday," whispered Fanny. "Does it still hurt?"

"It's a little bit tender," answered Sarah, with a toss of her head. "But I could play today if I were allowed out."

"I'm sorry," repeated Fanny. "It was a terrible thing to do. I lost my temper, I don't know why."

"I called you Fats once too often, that's why," answered Sarah. "I never thought you'd get mad and hit me. You never did before."

"You knew I did it on purpose?"

"Sure. You're too good a shot to miss the goal by that much. Besides, I saw you take aim at me."

Fanny hung her head. That's exactly what she had done, and it sounded so awful. "I'm not sure I'll ever play hockey again," she announced, swallowing hard.

"Don't be so foolish. Anyone could get mad. It's nothing." Fanny could hardly believe her ears. Sarah went on. "I can't see why you mind a nickname so much, though. Nearly all the men on the Famish Gut team have nicknames, like Joe the Hook, or Frank the Flash."

"Fatty is different."

"Oh, well, if you really mind, I won't call you that any more." Sarah was very offhand, but Fanny was too surprised to answer her. "But I wish you had a different name," Sarah went on. "Aunt Fanny Moore lives next door and I hate her. Ever since I can remember it's been, 'Don't touch my fence' or 'Don't play ball in front of my house'. I bet that woman has a dozen balls belonging to me. If one went in her yard, she grabbed it and never gave it back. And sometimes it wasn't easy to get another. I can't stand her, so I don't like the name."

They heard Sarah's mother come in and set down the water bucket in the porch. "Show me the arithmetic," hissed Sarah. Together they bent over the book.

"Jimmy, leave that jam alone," came a yell as Sarah's mother entered. "Sarah, what have you been doing? Look, the whole jar of jam is gone." Then Fanny saw that the little boy had his hand in the jam bottle and he was covered from his eyebrows to his chest. "Give me that," the mother went on angrily, grabbing the bottle and giving the boy a sharp slap. Instantly, he began roaring, waking the baby who joined in. "Why didn't you look after them, Sarah," her mother yelled. "I left you in charge."

"I'd better go," whispered Fanny, and she crept out as fast as she could, the loud voices following her. She scurried down the lane, glad to leave the noise and anger behind. For the first time in her life she felt sorry for Sarah, the oldest of five children in a messy house with a mother who yelled like that.

Back at the schoolyard she drew Millie aside. "I went to see Sarah and she's fine," she whispered.

"You went to her house!"

"Yes. I had to find out if she was alive. You knew I hit her on purpose?" Millie nodded. "It was a terrible thing to do, but she's not mad, and she's not really hurt."

"That's good. I was frightened. I thought she'd beat us up when she got back."

"No. I told her I was sorry, and she said if I hated Fatty, she wouldn't use it anymore. She'd call me Fanny."

Millie looked at her, eyes shining. "That's great. I expect she'll tell the others, too."

After school she thought and thought about her name. Sarah hated it, and she didn't really like it much herself. As soon as she got home, she said, "Mom, why did you call me Fanny?"

"It's a family name. Your father's sister that died was Fanny, and so was my mother, and two of your great-grandmothers."

"I don't like it much."

"Well, it's not exactly my favourite name. I wanted to call you Louise, but with all your grandparents expecting you to be called Fanny, your dad and I decided on Fanny Louise. And after all that, the minister we had then said Fanny was not a proper name, it was just a short form of Frances. Before we knew what was happening, he had dipped his fingers into the bowl of water and said, 'Frances Louise, I baptize you in the name of the Father, and of the Son, and of the Holy Ghost.' Remember that, Grandma, right there in the front room, with all of the relatives around?"

Grandma closed her lips in a firm line, then she said, "He didn't last long here, that minister, less than two years. Got people's back up, he did. Of course, we ignored him and called you Fanny."

The girl's eyes were shining. "You mean my name is really Frances? Can I tell anyone?"

"Of course, if you want to. I'll show you where it is entered in the family Bible. All right, Grandma?"

Grandmother nodded, and Mom went into the bedroom and came out carrying a huge Bible, not the one they used for family prayers, and opened it on the table.

Between the Old and New Testaments were several pages on which there was writing. "It starts here with your great-grandparents," said Mom, and Fanny read the first entry, written in beautiful, fine script, the ink faded: *Walter John*

Grace married Fanny Jane, daughter of John and Emily Grant, March 30, 1850.

"That's Grandpa's mother and father," said Mom.

There followed two pages of children born and baptized and then, on the top of the next page, she read: *James Edward Grace married Elizabeth Mary, daughter of Isaac and Fanny Moore, December 15, 1886.*

"That's you and Grandpa, isn't it, Gran?" Only two children were listed on that page: *A son, born March 1, 1888. Baptized Walter John, May 30, 1888. A daughter, born October 25, 1890. Baptized Fanny Elizabeth, March 16, 1891. Died November 10, 1892.*

"She was just a tiny girl, wasn't she, Gran?" Fanny said, hugging her grandmother. "I don't really mind being called Fanny."

"You'd better see your own entry, child."

They turned the page. At the top it said: *Walter John Grace married Edna Prudence, daughter of Thomas and Fanny Mitchell, May 20, 1914.*

After a space, there were two more entries: *A son, born February 12, 1917. Baptized James Edward May 16, 1917. A daughter, born June 5, 1919. Baptized Frances Louise, November 10, 1919.*

"Mom, you won't mind if some of the girls want to call me Frances?"

"It's your name, right there in the family Bible."

"But you and Gran and all the family can go on calling me Fanny."

"Thank you," said Mother drily.

And in no time at all Fatty Grace had disappeared. In her place there was Fanny, or Frances, or even Fran — all of which were pretty fine names.

10

The next September was such an exciting time. As Fanny and Millie walked west, they were joined by Margie Marsh, Betty Fairway, Jane Miller and, last of all, Sarah Thorne. These girls had gone together to the little one-room school till they were the biggest pupils there. Now they were to start again, in the lowest grade in the senior school. None of them admitted being scared, but Fanny suspected they all felt a little breathless, the way she did.

It was strange being in a room with only one grade, with a male teacher, and no recess. There was time for nothing at midday but to walk home, eat, and walk back.

But as soon as the ice on the pond was ready, those who lived far away brought a sandwich to eat at school so they had nearly an hour on their skates. One of the teachers was always in charge, but young men from Famish Gut coached the different hockey teams. They made up four junior girls' teams, and those teams practised every day.

Warren Marsh was proud of his girls for, when the time came, every one of them was named to the special team. There were three strings of forwards on the team that was finally chosen, along with two pairs for defence, and two goalies.

This was the team that was to represent Famish Gut and play other teams from nearby communities.

To Sarah's delight, she was to play left wing instead of defence for she was a fast skater and had a hard shot. She and Fanny had not become close friends, but they respected each other's ability. And as long as Fanny and Millie could keep up with her, and their passes were accurate, Sarah was pleasant enough.

The day for the first game came. All four teams from Famish Gut were bundled into sleighs to be driven to Rocky Harbour to compete. Dad drove their wonderful red side sleigh with Fanny, Millie, Jim and Frank all covered with blankets and a bearskin rug.

They gathered at the church hall in Rocky Harbour and drank the hot cocoa the Ladies' Aid had provided. The junior girls were to play first. Fanny's fingers trembled with nervousness as she laced on her skates. For the very first time in her life, she was part of a team that represented her home community.

A great crowd had gathered to watch. Most of them would cheer for Rocky Harbour, Fanny knew. But, as she went on the ice to warm up before the game, she realized that on one side of the rink were the other three teams from Famish Gut and all the sleigh drivers, about sixty altogether. She smiled at her father and at Warren Marsh, who called encouragement to the team.

The whistle blew. Sarah, Fanny and Millie were to begin the game; no one said so, but Fanny felt sure they were the best forward line. She went to centre for the face-off, her knees almost trembling with nervousness. She got the draw and flicked the puck to Sarah. Away the three went up the ice, but in her eagerness Sarah got ahead and her pass to Millie, just out of reach, was grabbed by the Rocky Harbour defence, and away the play went back to the other end.

After a few moments, the lines were changed and Fanny, tense and breathing hard, watched from the sidelines. The third string from each team was on the ice when a hard shot from just inside the blueline was deflected and sailed past Lily Moore into the Famish Gut net.

The Rocky Harbour crowd cheered wildly. Tom Green, their coach, said very quietly behind them, "First string, get out there and score." As Fanny took her place at centre ice for the face-off, the freckled redhaired girl opposite her said, "Famish Gut." She curled her lip and stuck her nose in the air, as if there was a bad smell. "Famish Gut — hah!" she sneered.

Fanny felt her cheeks burn. I'll think of something nasty to say to her, she determined. The whistle sounded, the puck was dropped, and again Fanny flicked it to Sarah. Up and down they raced, trying not to pull back too far, but making sure not to leave their defence too open.

Fanny's mind was not altogether on the game all the time. It seemed to her that whenever she was on the ice in that first period, the redhead was there too, sniffing and saying "Famish Gut!" whenever she came near. Fanny got more and more angry; she could feel the blood pounding in her head. Then, as she rushed up the ice and was about to slam the puck almost blindly towards the goal, she heard, "Fran! Fran!" She turned, laid the puck right on her partner's stick, and immediately Sarah deflected it into the net.

It was the turn of the Famish Gut fans to cheer. Fanny was very pleased with herself. You keep your temper, she told herself, and you'll help triumph over that redhead by beating her team.

71

As their line went off the ice, Sarah said, "I was afraid you weren't going to get the puck to me. I didn't think you saw me in the clear, practically on the goal crease."

"I didn't," answered Fanny, "but I heard you."

In spite of her resolution, that was their only goal in the first period, which ended in a tie. Tom talked to them at the interval. "We can beat them," he said. "But my first string is not passing as much as usual. You two, Sarah and Fanny, have tried shooting three or four times when Millie was in a better position and you should have passed. Try to play as a team, the way you do at home."

The three exchanged glances. I don't know about Sarah, thought Fanny, but I've been trying too hard to score on my own, just to show that snooty girl.

Early in the second period the third string from Famish Gut scored. Fanny was glad because they had been on the ice when Rocky Harbour had scored and this evened things up for them. Then the first string was back on the ice, and Fanny forgot the sneering enemy and everything else, except to play as she did at home, cruising in front of the goal every chance she got.

But it was Millie who scored. Fanny faked a shot and passed the puck to her friend who was in the clear, and Millie made no mistake. The second period ended three-to-one.

The third period was a triumph. Fanny, with the help of her wings, scored three unanswered goals and the deafening roar from her side of the rink as the game ended was sweet music in her ears. When the teams gathered on the ice to cheer each other, she had no trouble resisting the temptation to stick out her tongue at the redhead. Fanny already had her revenge.

On Monday morning the principal talked to the whole school. "We had a good day on Saturday," he said. "True, our senior girls were beaten two-to-one, and our junior boys four-to-two, but our senior boys played fine hockey, winning five-to-two over Rocky Harbour. And we were especially pleased with our junior girls. One string in particular, composed of Sarah Thorne, Frances Grace, and Mildred King, all pupils in their first year at this school, played exceptionally fine hockey. We look for great things from them this year, and every year that they are in school. Famish Gut is proud of you all, and of the fine spirit of good sport you displayed."

Fanny was so pleased and proud she didn't notice that Famish Gut sounded awful. And they did have a good year, the junior girls' team in particular. Of the nine games they played against Rocky Harbour, Cheerful Cove and Dent's Bight, they won eight and tied one. Famish Gut was as proud of them as they were of the senior men who went on winning the championship year after year.

11

Spring came. The ice disappeared. And the muddy roads were back. Competition over, the girls concentrated more on their school work and their examinations. Fanny had no trouble here and, instead of being glad when Sarah and Jane found their mathematics difficult, she helped them as best she could on the way to school.

One dull windy morning, she came downstairs to find only her mother and grandmother at the table. This was strange, for now that woodcutting was finished her grandfather was usually there.

"He went out just after daylight this morning," said Grandma. "My rheumatism was bothering me last night, and I kept waking him up, I suppose. Anyway, around three he got up to get me the linament, and of course he looked out the window at the weather. He thought he saw the lights of a ship not far off the harbour mouth, and expected to see her safely at anchor this morning. But she's not in the harbour, and it was a pretty wild night. So, he's climbing up on the headland to have a look out to sea. I didn't want him to go climbing up there, but he's a stubborn old man."

"Do you think he imagined the lights, Grandma?"

"No, child, and I don't think they were the kind of lights

Uncle Tom White saw, either. But there are lots of good harbours near where a ship might anchor.'

Just then Dad rushed in. "There's a big ship aground on the reef just outside the harbour mouth," he said. "We have to get down the cliff on ropes and throw them a line. Get Jim up, and Fanny, you and he get all the men out. You take the first eight or ten houses, and let Jim start at Miller's. Tell the men to bring ropes to the cliff, and tell the women to get ready to dry clothes for the sailors and to feed them."

"Get going, Fanny. I'll call Jim," said Mother.

So Fanny put on her boots and warm coat, and ran next door, giving Dad's message. She had finished three houses when Jim raced past her. Soon men were running towards the cliff, pulling on jackets as they went, carrying coils of rope.

When Fanny had finished her houses, she began to climb the path to the cliff, and was joined by Millie and Dottie. They walked , bent over, the wind almost snatching their breath away. Soon the path petered out and there was nothing between them and the jagged headland except bare slippery rocks with little patches of moss. "I can't go any further," panted Dottie. "I can hardly breathe."

They paused, looking towards the point. Men were still making their way upward, slipping, stumbling, their clothes ballooning in the fierce gale. Millie crouched low, her back to the hurricane winds, and the other two did the same. "We don't need to climb all the way out to the point," she gasped. "If we could get to the edge of the ridge we'd be able to see the water and the reef, wouldn't we?"

Fanny nodded. One behind the other, they made their way on hands and knees over the rough ground till they could look down on the dark angry ocean. Crouched close together, they turned to the right.

There, on a jagged reef that stretched from the north point of the harbour mouth, was a big ship keeled over on its side, its deck half awash. Towering waves rushed in and broke against it and against the black rocks, sending a huge spray of foam into the air to fall back over the tiny figures clinging to the deck.

"I can see a rope reaching from the ship to the foot of the cliff," said Dottie.

Fanny didn't answer. Her eyes were on two men out on the dark slippery rocks, halfway between ship and shore. "That's my father," she said solemnly. "My dad is away out there on the reef."

"You can't tell from here," protested Millie.

"Yes, I can. I know it's Dad in his yellow oilskins. Look, he's helping that man in over the rocks."

Sure enough, a sailor who had made his way, hand over hand, clinging to the rope, was hauled up on the rocks by the two Famish Gut men who waited away out on the reef. After a pause the seaman went on his way towards the foot of the cliffs to be hauled up by those waiting at the top. Meanwhile, Fanny's father and the others on the reef were dragging the next sailor out of the pounding waves.

A number of men who had been hauled to the top of the cliff were slowly making their way down toward the houses, and the Famish Gut children were waiting to meet them. Each child would seize a half-drowned exhausted man by the arm and take him home to be warmed, dried, and fed.

"We'd better go and help the sailors," said Dottie. And so they did.

Fanny led one almost exhausted young man to her house and left him in the care of her mother and grandmother. She then went outside and watched other children and strangers go by. She didn't climb back to the edge of the cliff to look down at her own father, out on the slippery reef, half-drowned in the salty spray. She told herself that he would be safe; he was used to the sea. Besides, he probably had a rope anchoring him safely, though she hadn't been able to see one. Still, she strained her eyes as the Famish Gut men began to come back. At last she saw her grandfather. "Where's Dad?" she shouted to him. "Where's my father?"

"He's coming. He's helping to see to a young fellow whose leg was crushed. Run and tell your mother to fix up a bed on the kitchen couch. This one is barely alive."

By the time Dad and Will King had gotten the injured man to the kitchen, a place had been made comfortable with quilts and pillows. Fanny noticed that the man's leg had splints fastened from hip to ankle. Half unconscious, his wet clothes were stripped off and he was made snug and warm on his makeshift bed.

"See if you can get him to swallow some strong sweet tea," said Grandma. Then she turned to Dad, stripping off his yellow oilskins. "Is everyone safe?"

"Yes, and the minister is phoning the hospital in St. John's to see if they will send an ambulance out for this man, and another whose arm was crushed." Dad went off to his bedroom to change.

That afternoon most of the children of Famish Gut crowded around a white ambulance, the first they had ever seen, and watched while a young doctor supervised getting the injured men on board.

Close behind the ambulance came a car with a news reporter and a cameraman. They wanted to be shown the wreck, and the cliff up which the sailors had been dragged to safety. A number of men showed them where it was, and told the details of the rescue.

While the photographer was getting shots of the scene, the reporter went to the railway station where most of the sailors were gathering to take the train, and got their story. Then he walked along the road, talking to adults and children.

It was all terribly exciting. No child could remember anything important enough to get into the St. John's papers happening in Famish Gut before. Fanny was almost bursting with pride when she saw her father and grandfather having their picture taken.

The next morning in church the minister said a special prayer of thanksgiving that they had been given the opportunity of saving men from a watery grave. Fanny smiled to herself as she thought of Gran's rheumatism. The minister ought to be saying a special thank you for that, otherwise, no one would have known that the wreck was there.

On Tuesday Jim came home from school excitedly waving a newspaper addressed to Grandfather. There, on the front page, was a picture of the wreck on the reef and, inside, some of the people. There was a big one of Dad and Grandfather, looking just like themselves: Dad was grinning rather sheepishly, and Grandpa was serious, almost scowling, as usual.

The whole family sat and listened as Mom read the account of the daring rescue by the heroic men of Famish Gut. At least, that's what the paper said.

"That reporter made it sound like something wonderful we did," said Dad. "Anyone would throw a rope and haul men up the cliff. It was nothing special."

"He's a landlubber, my son; he knows nothing about ropes or the sea," scoffed Grandfather. Then he continued softly, "Let me see that picture again, Edna."

Fanny stood at her grandfather's side and looked at the spread of pictures on the middle page of the newspaper. "Famish Gut heroes of daring rescue" was the caption under the picture of the two Grace men.

Grandpa turned to look at her, and there was almost a twinkle in his eye. "You know, Fanny, I'm just as glad you didn't change the name of this place."

Fanny smiled. She tried to imagine her grandfather as a Fairy Glen hero, but she couldn't. Somehow Famish Gut sounded like a proper place for a daring rescue of shipwrecked sailors. She nodded at her grandfather, then turned to hug her grandmother, making sure not to bump her swollen ankles.